All About Sea Turtles

Katie Gillespie

EYEDISCOVER

EYEDISCOVER

Go to **www.eyediscover.com** and enter this book's unique code.

BOOK CODE

X 5 9 7 4 2 3

EYEDISCOVER brings you media enhanced books that support active learning.

Published by AV² by Weigl
350 5th Avenue, 59th Floor   New York, NY   10118
Website: www.eyediscover.com

Library of Congress Control Number: 2016932937

ISBN 978-1-4896-5176-1 (hardcover)

Printed in the United States of America
in Brainerd, Minnesota
1 2 3 4 5 6 7 8 9 0   20 19 18 17 16

032016
030416

Editor: Katie Gillespie
Designer: Mandy Christiansen

Weigl acknowledges Getty Images, Corbis, Alamy, and Shutterstock as the primary image suppliers for this title.

EYEDISCOVER provides enriched content, optimized for tablet use, that supplements and complements this book. EYEDISCOVER books strive to create inspired learning and engage young minds in a total learning experience.

Watch
Video content brings each page to life.

Browse
Thumbnails make navigation simple.

Read
Follow along with text on the screen.

I am the king of the jungle.

Listen
Hear each page read aloud.

Your EYEDISCOVER Optic Readalongs come alive with...

Audio
Listen to the entire book read aloud.

Video
High resolution videos turn each spread into an optic readalong.

OPTIMIZED FOR

☑ **TABLETS**

☑ **WHITEBOARDS**

☑ **COMPUTERS**

☑ **AND MUCH MORE!**

All About Sea Turtles

In this book, you will learn about

- how they look

- where they live

- what they eat

and much more!

Sea turtles are reptiles with shells on their backs. They live in oceans all over the world.

There are seven different kinds of sea turtles. Kemp's ridleys are the smallest and leatherbacks are the largest.

The first sea turtles lived on Earth before most dinosaurs.

9

Sea turtles spend most of their time alone. They only come together to find a mate or look for food.

Sea turtles travel very far to nest. They go back to the beaches where they were born.

13

Mother sea turtles dig holes in the sand and lay their eggs inside.

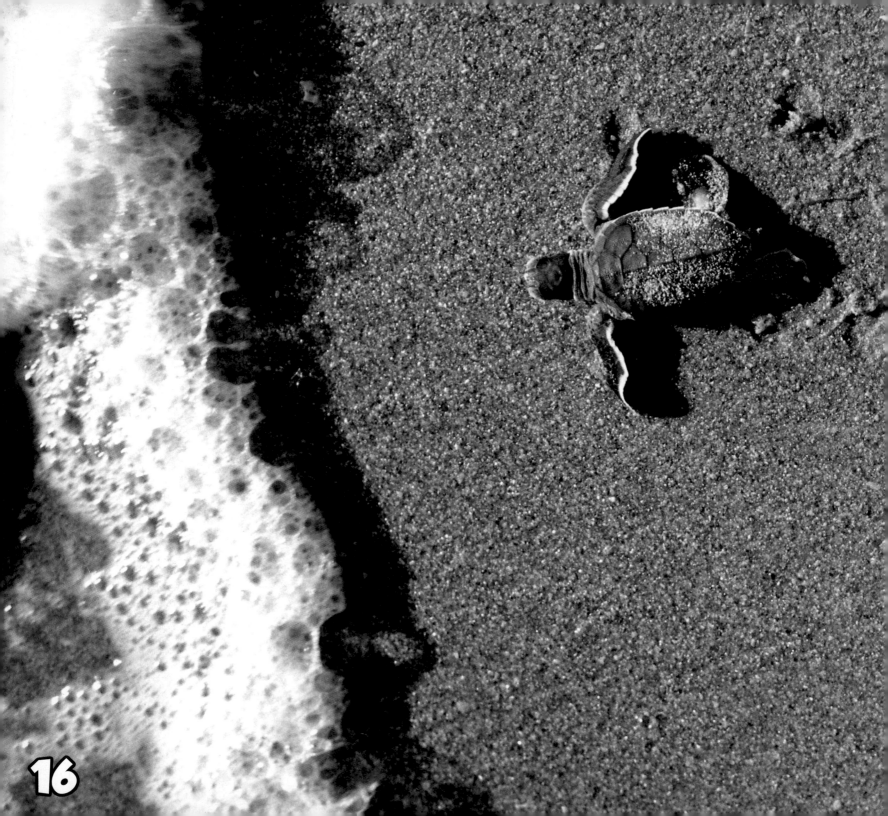

16

Baby sea turtles are called hatchlings. They go back to the ocean after hatching from their eggs.

Sea turtles can eat plants or animals. Some sea turtles eat both.

Sea turtles can live for more than 100 years. It is important for people to leave them alone.

SEA TURTLES BY THE NUMBERS

Hatchlings
are about the size of
a cookie
at birth.

Sea turtles
are found in
every ocean except
the **Arctic.**

**Some sea
turtles**
lay up to

200
eggs at
a time.

Sea turtles can swim at

SPEEDS

of more than
20 miles per hour.
(32 kilometers per hour)

A **sea turtle** can
slow its heartbeat to
one beat every
9 minutes
while diving.

Green
sea turtles can
hold their breath
under water for up to

5

hours.

Leatherbacks

can weigh as much

as a

pickup truck.

KEY WORDS

Research has shown that as much as 65 percent of all written material published in English is made up of 300 words. These 300 words cannot be taught using pictures or learned by sounding them out. They must be recognized by sight. This book contains 56 common sight words to help young readers improve their reading fluency and comprehension. This book also teaches young readers several important content words, such as proper nouns. These words are paired with pictures to aid in learning and improve understanding.

Page	Sight Words First Appearance	Page	Content Words First Appearance
4	all, are, backs, in, live, on, over, sea, the, their, they, with, world	4	oceans, reptiles, sea turtles, shells
7	and, different, kinds, of, there	7	Kemp's ridleys, leatherbacks
8	before, Earth, first, most	8	dinosaurs
11	a, come, find, food, for, look, only, or, time, to, together	12	beaches
12	far, go, very, were, where	14	eggs, holes, sand
14	mother	17	baby, hatchlings
17	after, from		
18	animals, both, can, eat, plants, some		
21	important, is, it, leave, more, people, than, them, years		

Watch
Video content brings each page to life.

Browse
Thumbnails make navigation simple.

Read
Follow along with text on the screen.

I am the king of the jungle.

Listen
Hear each page read aloud.

EYEDISCOVER

Go to **www.eyediscover.com** and enter this book's unique code.

BOOK CODE

X597423